A Neal Porter Book
ROARING BROOK PRESS
New York

By Ed Galing

Illustrated by Erin E. Stead

By Ed Galing

Illustrated by Erin E. Stead

A Neal Porter Book

ROARING BROOK PRESS

New York

Tony

that was his name

he was such a
wonderful horse

and pulled a milk
truck
for Tom, the young
driver

Tom Jones,
in the early hours of the
morning,

pulling the wagon loaded
with milk, butter,
and eggs,

Tony was all white,
large, sturdy,
with wide gentle eyes
and a ton of love,

he would wait patiently
while Tom jumped off the
wagon to put my
milk and eggs on
my doorstep,

it was early in the morning
around three a.m.,
but I was up, and would
go out and pat Tony with
my gentle arms, and
his head would bow down
and his eyes would glow

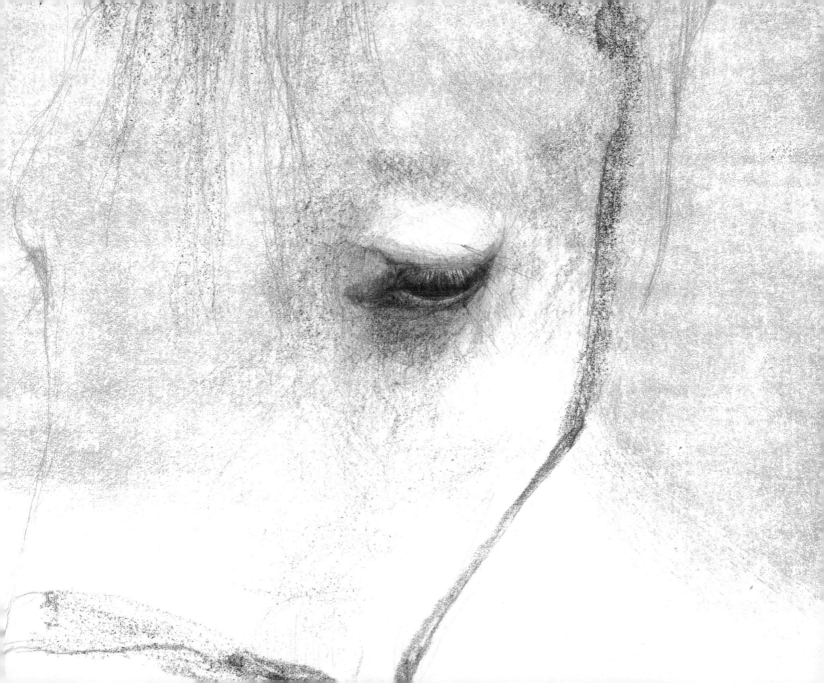

and Tom would say
nice to see you out so early,
sir,
and Tony always looks
for you too,

wouldn't miss Tony for the world,
I would reply
sturdily,
giving Tony another pat,

he is such a wonderful
horse, and so handsome.

I am sure he heard
that, Tom would
smile widely,
as he got back into
the truck

and as they pulled away

I knew that Tony
did a little dance.

For my dad —E.S.

Text copyright © 2017 by Ed Galing

Illustrations copyright © 2017 by Erin E. Stead

A Neal Porter Book

Published by Roaring Brook Press

Roaring Brook Press is a division of Holtzbrinck Publishing Holdings Limited Partnership

175 Fifth Avenue, New York, New York 10010

The art for this book was created using Gomuban monoprinting and pencil.

mackids.com

Library of Congress Control Number: 2016942447

ISBN: 978-1-62672-308-5

Our books may be purchased in bulk for promotional, educational, or business use. Please
contact your local bookseller or the Macmillan Corporate and Premium Sales Department
at (800) 221-7945 ext. 5442 or by e-mail at MacmillanSpecialMarkets@macmillan.com.

First edition 2017

Printed in China by RR Donnelley Asia Printing Solutions Ltd., Dongguan City, Guangdong Province

1   3   5   7   9   10   8   6   4   2